MAYBE
MAYBE
MARISOL
RAINEY

ERIN ENTRADA KELLY

MAYBE MAYBE

MARISOL
RAINEY

GREENWILLOW BOOKS

An Imprint of HarperCollinsPublishers

Maybe Maybe Marisol Rainey.
Copyright © 2021 by Erin Entrada Kelly

The text of this book is set in Garth Graphic. Book design by Sylvie Le Floc'h

Library of Congress Cataloging-in-Publication Data

Names: Kelly, Erin Entrada, author.
Title: Maybe maybe Marisol Rainey / Erin Entrada Kelly.
Description: First edition. | New York : Greenwillow Books, [2021] | Audience: Ages 8-12. | Audience: Grades 2-3. | Summary: "Marisol, who has a big imagination and likes to name inanimate objects, has a tree in her backyard named Peppina... but she's way too scared to climb it. Will Marisol find the courage to climb Peppina? Maybe"—Provided by publisher.
Identifiers: LCCN 2021002253 | ISBN 9780062970428 (hardback) | ISBN 9780062970442 (ebook)
Subjects: CYAC: Imagination—Fiction. | Courage—Fiction. | Magnolias—Fiction. | Trees—Fiction. | Best friends—Fiction. | Friendship—Fiction.
Classification: LCC PZ7.1.K45 May 2021 | DDC [Fic]—dc23
LC record available at https://lccn.loc.gov/2021002253

21 22 23 24 25 PC/LSCH 10 9 8 7 6 5 4 3 2 1
First Edition
Greenwillow Books

For Peanut

CONTENTS

THE TREE IS NAMED PEPPINA

There is a magnolia tree in Marisol Rainey's backyard. The tree is named Peppina. It is perfect for climbing. The branches are practically *made* for human feet. It's as if Peppina wanted to say: *Step here, and here, and here.*

Peppina has a thick branch close to the ground, like she's giving you a boost. Marisol calls this booster branch. There's another one just above it, like a step with a knob in it. She calls this knobby branch. Peppina also has a canopy of dense, rubbery leaves that shield you from the Louisiana sun and make it easy to hide when you don't want to be found.

Marisol is the one who named her. She got the name from an old movie called *Poor Little Peppina*, starring Mary Pickford. She watched the movie on her first night in the new house. The next day, Marisol was exploring the backyard. She'd never had a backyard. They'd lived in an apartment before they moved to their house last year. She stood on the root of the magnolia tree, craned her neck to give it a good once-over, and said, "Hello, Peppina."

She didn't say it in a friendly way.

She didn't say it in a cheerful way.

Think of someone you're never happy to see, like your dentist, or the principal after you're sent to the office.

That's how Marisol said "Hello, Peppina."

Like she was greeting a bowl of cold oatmeal.

Marisol was the only person who felt this way. Everyone else thought Peppina was the perfect tree.

Well, maybe not *everyone*, since there are millions of people who have never met Peppina. But according to Marisol's big brother, Oz, who is twelve, Peppina is the "best tree ever."

"This is the best tree ever!" said Oz, the first time he climbed it. He climbed up, up, up, past booster branch, past knobby branch, all the way up, until he was so high he had to lean forward to peer down at Marisol, whose heart went *thump, thump, thump.*

Sometimes Oz's best friend, Stu, would come over, and they'd scurry up the tree like squirrels.

Small shards of bark and leaves would rain down from Peppina as their sneakers went up, up, up. Marisol told herself that they were able to climb it so easily because they were older, but even Jada George—Marisol's best friend since last year— loved Peppina.

"This is the best tree ever!" said Jada, the first time she climbed Peppina.

Once—and only once—Marisol's orange cat, Jelly Beans, climbed the tree and wouldn't come down for six hours. Marisol cried until her eyes hurt. She imagined Beans stuck there forever. But when Beans finally came down, he looked perfectly content, as if he'd spent all day at the beach.

Everyone loved Peppina.

Everyone but Marisol.

THE THING
ABOUT BEST FRIENDS

It's the first day of summer, and it's approximately five bazillion degrees outside, with 2,000 percent humidity. That's how summers are in Louisiana.

"When I grow up, I'm going to move somewhere that isn't so hot all the time," says Jada. She's lying on Peppina's booster branch with one leg dangling down. One of the best things about Jada is that she lives only three blocks away, so she can ride her bike over anytime, except when she spends weekends with her dad.

Marisol is planted on the ground. She's listening to the birds. She loves the way they chirp to each other. She wonders what they're saying. *It must be exciting to be a bird,* she thinks.

"Where would you go, if you could go anywhere?" Marisol asks.

"I don't know. Maybe Athens."

"Where is Athens?"

"In Greece."

"Isn't it hot in Greece, too?" Marisol asks.

"I'm not sure," says Jada. "We'll ask your mom."

Jada and Marisol agree that Mrs. Rainey is the smartest person they know. In addition to teaching seventh-grade science, Mrs. Rainey speaks three languages: English, Spanish, and Tagalog, which is the language of the Philippines, where Mrs. Rainey was born.

Jada and Marisol only speak English, but sometimes they learn words in other languages so no one will know what they're saying.

When Mrs. Ruby told them they'd have to give book reports in front of the class last year, for example, Marisol leaned over and whispered "furchtbar" to Jada, which means "terrible" in German. Marisol hated speaking in front of the class. It made her stomach twist in knots. It made her palms sweat. It made her heart beat fast. And when she got up in front of everyone, her paper shook in her hand. Her voice shook, too. And annoying Evie Smythe, who volunteered to give her book reports first because she just couldn't *wait,* pointed out Marisol's shakiness to everyone.

One of the things Marisol loves most about Jada is that she never makes fun of her for being scared. Even right now, Jada doesn't mind that Marisol has never climbed Peppina.

"When I get to Athens, I'm going to wander the streets and yell my ideas at everyone," says Jada. Dangle, dangle. "Just like Socrates."

THERE is only ONE good
—KnowLeDge!!
There is ONLY ONE evil
— ignorance!!

ICE cream for BREAKFAST!!

JAdA aND SOCRaTES yell thEiR ideas at peopLe.

People didn't like Socrates very much, so they made him drink hemlock, which is a type of poison. Sometimes Jada and Marisol would pretend to drink poison at the Raineys' dinner table. They'd clutch their throats and collapse out of their chairs, right onto the floor. Only it wasn't really poison. Usually it was pineapple juice.

"Where do you want to live when you grow up?" Jada asks.

Marisol leans her head against Peppina and thinks of other places in the world. Places that are not Getty, Louisiana. First she imagines the Philippines, because that's where her mother was born. Her mom has told her many stories of the Philippines—the bright, beautiful ocean and the big, round mangoes. Marisol hasn't been there yet, but she can picture it.

Maybe I can live there, she thinks. *Maybe.*

But then she remembers all her relatives. She has many aunts, uncles, and cousins in the Philippines whom she has never met. *If I move there,* Marisol thinks, *I'll have to meet them all at once.* She imagines them gathered together in a swollen crowd, waiting for her with wide, curious eyes.

They can't wait to swarm her with hugs and kisses. She sees herself stepping off the plane or boat or whatever, holding a suitcase. She doesn't know what to do or say. Her hands get sweaty. She disappears into the swarm, and it's a friendly swarm, but she doesn't know how to act, because even though they are aunts and uncles and cousins, she doesn't really *know* them.

She decides she should visit first. Meet people one by one, instead of all at once.

She imagines New York instead. But then she hears the car horns blaring and sees all the lights in Times Square burning and feels all the people bumping into her on the sidewalks. What if she got lost in all that noise or didn't cross the street at the right time and got hit by a bus?

She imagines Paris, but all she knows about
Paris is the Eiffel Tower, which is very tall. Much
taller than Peppina. What if she fell off the top
of the Eiffel Tower? What then? She'd become a
crêpe on the sidewalk, that's what.

Crêpe is French for "pancake."

Eiffel Tower
1,063 FEEt ←

Pepping
↓ 40 feet

Jada puts an imaginary walkie-talkie to her mouth and turns it on.

"Jada to Marisol, Jada to Marisol," she says.

"I was trying to think of someplace to live, but I couldn't think of anywhere," says Marisol.

"That's okay. You can live with me in Athens," says Jada. "Or we can stay here. We can live in this tree. And no one will know where we are, because Peppina always has leaves, even in the winter. Everyone would be, like, whatever happened to Jada and Marisol? And we'd be up here, like spies."

Marisol uses the sleeve of her T-shirt to wipe the sweat from her forehead. "I can't live in Peppina, because I don't climb trees," she says quietly.

"That's okay," Jada says. "We can always live on the ground."

That's the thing about best friends. They don't care about all the things you can't do.

"Maybe I'll climb it one day, though," says Marisol.

Maybe.

THE THING
ABOUT PEPPINA

Here's the thing about Peppina.

Peppina is very tall, and Marisol's legs are very short.

The ground underneath Peppina is very hard, and Marisol's head is very delicate.

Marisol has two skinny arms, but Peppina has hundreds of thick branches, none of which can catch her if she falls.

Marisol wants to climb Peppina. She wants to know what it's like to see the world from way up high. She wants to dangle one leg down and swing it back and forth like Jada does. But every time she pictures it, she sees herself falling.

Falling is one of Marisol's greatest fears. Not just from trees, either.

When Marisol goes down stairs, she grips the handrail and concentrates on every step.

When it's time to ride escalators, she takes deep breaths before she steps forward.

The only time she isn't afraid of slipping and falling is when she goes down the slides at school or in the park, but that's because slides are made for slipping and falling.

Stairs are not.

Escalators are not.

Trees certainly are not.

BUSTER, SCRAPS, AND SERFS

The best part about coming inside from the backyard is the air-conditioning. It makes you want to collapse on the floor until every bead of sweat has turned nice and cool. Marisol and Jada grab their favorite cups (Marisol's is green; Jada's is red) and fill them with cold water from a pitcher in the refrigerator. Beans darts in. Beans meows once at Marisol. The meow means "I'm so glad you're back, Marisol. I missed you greatly."

When Marisol finishes her water, she lays

her hand on the refrigerator and says, "Thanks, Buster." Then she reaches down to scratch Beans's ears.

Buster is the name of the refrigerator. His full name is Buster Keaton. Marisol named him after the actor Buster Keaton, who was known as

BUSTER Keaton, Actor →

BUSTER Keaton, REFRigeratoR →

"The Great Stone Face," because he didn't have many expressions. There was a lot happening under the surface, though. It's the same with the refrigerator. Strange humming noises. Lights that go on and off when you open and close the doors. An ice maker that churns and grunts.

Refrigerators don't usually have names like Buster, just as trees don't normally have names like Peppina. But Marisol believes that all things—all important things, anyway—should have their own names. She wouldn't want to be called "human" or "girl," after all. Why should it be any different for refrigerators and trees?

Jada is the only one who knows about Marisol's names for things. Marisol would never tell Oz. Not in a million years. And she'd never tell her dad, because he wouldn't understand. He already thought she was too sensitive. He'd once killed a spider in their old apartment, and Marisol had cried until she got the hiccups.

"Oh, Scraps," he'd said. Scraps was his nickname for her. "One day you'll be out in the big, bad world. You can't be so sensitive."

Jada doesn't think it's weird that Marisol named the refrigerator.

When Jada finishes her water, she says, "Thanks, Buster." Just like Marisol.

✺ ✺

Jada and Marisol enjoy spying on people. Like the Raineys' neighbor, Mr. Zhang, who keeps bees in his backyard. Or Mrs. Rainey, even though all she does is read mystery novels, grade lab reports, and watch animal documentaries on television.

They can't spy on Mr. Rainey because he works on an oil rig in the Gulf of Mexico, and he is only home for one week every month.

Oz is their favorite person to spy on, because spying on Oz is a dangerous mission.

Today Oz's door is closed, but they know what he is doing. He is playing a video game called *Knights of Redemption*. They know he's playing *Knights of Redemption* because that's what he's always doing.

They tiptoe toward his bedroom door, holding their invisible walkie-talkies. Beans—not a good spy—sprawls on the floor between them and decides to take a nap.

Their first order of business is to open the target's door without him noticing.

Marisol reaches up—slowly, slowly—and lays her hand on the doorknob. Then she turns it—slowly, slowly. Her heart pounds in her ears.

She opens the door just a crack. She and Jada stay crouched and exchange looks that say *shh, quiet, quiet.*

Oz has his headset on. He's talking to his friends, who are also playing *Knights of Redemption.*

Oz is yelling: "That is so *not* cool, Stu! Not cool!"

Stu Smythe is Oz's best friend. He is also Evie Smythe's older brother, so Marisol isn't sure if she likes Oz being best friends with him. Not that she has a choice. Stu's real name is Stuart. Oz's real name is Osgood, but he says "Osgood" sounds like the name of a ninety-year-old man, and he'd rather be called Oz.

Marisol likes the name Osgood, because it's unique.

She likes the name Oz for the same reason.

"I *just* got that sword!" Oz shouts. Then he says a bad word. Not a really bad word, but a medium-bad word.

Marisol and Jada look at each other. Jada can't help it—she laughs.

Somehow—even with the loud video game, even with his headset on, even with the sounds of Stu's voice booming in his ears—Oz hears Jada's giggle.

Unlike Mrs. Rainey or Mr. Zhang, Oz has supersonic hearing when it comes to nosy little sisters.

"You have five seconds to get away from that door before I send a horde of fighting horses after you!" Oz yells, without getting up from his beanbag chair. "I know you're out there, serfs!"

Marisol wonders if there was really such a thing as fighting horses in the Middle Ages. She closes Oz's door and rushes into her bedroom with Jada right behind her. They collapse on the bed and laugh.

Beans opens one eye, then goes back to sleep.

DADHEAD

Even though Mr. Rainey is gone most of the time, Marisol and Oz see him every Monday, Wednesday, and Friday nights. He calls promptly at 7:00 p.m. When Mrs. Rainey's laptop chimes from the dining room table, Oz cries out: "Dadhead! Dadhead!"

Oz calls him Dadhead since it's always just his head on the computer screen.

Mr. Rainey is an electrician on an oil rig. He takes a choppy helicopter ride to get there. He says the Gulf of Mexico looks huge and endless when you're standing on an oil rig. When Marisol tries to imagine it, her stomach twists in knots.

DAD HEAD

It's 7:00 p.m., and Marisol, Oz, and Mrs. Rainey are all gathered around Dadhead. Even though they can only see his head and shoulders, Marisol can tell he's wearing his blue work coveralls. There is a sink behind him because he sets up his laptop in the rig's mess hall, which is what they call the dining room. So they're all together at a table, except one table is on Watkins Street in Getty, Louisiana, and the other one is in the middle of the Gulf of Mexico.

When Dadhead asks Oz and Marisol what they've been up to, Oz launches into a series of stories about soccer practice before Marisol can even open her mouth.

Finally it's her turn.

"I learned how to ride my bike without holding the handlebars," she says. "And I'm not even scared when I do it."

Mrs. Rainey frowns. "I don't think it's a good idea to ride your bike without holding on."

"I only let go for two seconds," Marisol says.

"That's pretty brave, Scraps, but your mother is right," Dadhead says. "Besides, if you don't hold on, you might get *two-tired* from riding." He pauses.

"Get it? Two-tired? Because bikes have two tires?"

Oz groans and shakes his head.

Mrs. Rainey says, "Good one, Will."

Marisol smiles. She smiles at his kind-of funny joke, and because he called her Scraps. She likes when her father calls her that. It feels like a gift just for her. The name came from a movie they saw together called *A Dog's Life*. The movie was really, *really* old—all the way from 1918. They saw it by accident on one of the weekends he was home. He'd promised to take her to the movies, and he'd promised she could see any movie she wanted, as long as it was PG.

When they reached the ticket counter, the movie they planned to see was sold out. They considered the other movies. Marisol immediately saw one she liked.

"Let's see *A Dog's Life*," Marisol said.

Dad squinted at the board. "I've never even heard of it." He looked at the guy behind the ticket counter. The guy had a name tag that said DANIEL on his shirt. "Who's in it?"

"Charlie Chaplin," Daniel said.

"Charlie Chaplin?" Dad repeated. "Are you serious?"

"Today is Sunday," Daniel replied. He tapped on the glass between them, at a flyer that said SILENT FILM SUNDAYS! "On the first Sunday of every month, we show a silent film."

Marisol had never heard of Charlie Chaplin or silent films. She just wanted to see a movie with a dog in it.

As it turned out, Charlie Chaplin had once been a huge star. Back then, they didn't know how to

put sound in movies. So they made movies where the characters never talked. Instead, someone in the movie theater played piano music while the actors acted out the scenes on the screen. Marisol loved *A Dog's Life.* It was about a poor and hungry man—played by Charlie Chaplin—who rescues a stray dog named Scraps.

Every now and then, Dad dozed off. When Scraps came on the screen, Marisol would nudge his arm and whisper, "Dad, it's Scraps!" She didn't really need to whisper, though, because they were the only ones in the theater.

Dad would open his eyes and say, "Your name is Scraps? I thought we named you Marisol."

And that was that.

scraps

A SCEnE FROM
"A DOg's Life"

TREETOP MARISOL

Marisol can't sleep.

Her bedtime is 8:45 p.m. sharp. That's when she and Beans have to be in bed with the lights out. Marisol is tucked under her bedspread, surrounded by cats. Her bedsheets are decorated with cats dressed in different costumes—here's one wearing a Victorian gown, here's another with a top hat, and there's one in a three-piece suit. Her pillow is shaped like a cat, with a real-life cat— Beans—curled next to it. She even has four stuffed animal cats lined up next to her. Their names are Nacho, Banana Split, Lumpia, and Pot Roast. She named them after her favorite foods.

Marisol feels very snug and cozy, but her mind races like a runaway train.

She is thinking of Peppina, wondering what it's like to be a tree. She imagines Peppina, standing proud and tall in the backyard, thinking, *How come everyone loves to climb me but Marisol?*

I'm sorry, Peppina, thinks Marisol. *I really want to. Maybe one day. Maybe.*

Then she imagines that she's not in her room at all. Instead, she's outside. It's a bright, sunny afternoon. She bounds across the backyard as fast as she can, then hoists herself up on Peppina's booster branch. And she doesn't stop there. Up, up, she goes. She doesn't even worry about scraping her knees. She is the fastest tree climber in the state, maybe the whole world. Up, up. She's not scared at all. She pokes her head out of the very top of the tree; because she's so high, she has nowhere else to go. It isn't spring, but she can smell the magnolias, and she isn't even sneezing.

Suddenly the whole neighborhood gathers around Peppina. They all shade their eyes with their hands and get on their tiptoes, trying to see

Marisol, the fastest and bravest tree climber in the world. She waves and yells, "Look at me!" Everyone oohs and aahs. Jada is down there, too. She's smiling so wide that Marisol can see all her top teeth, even from here. And there's Evie Smythe with her arms crossed. She's jealous because Marisol is getting so much attention.

"See, Evie? I bet *you* can't make it all the way up here!" Marisol calls to her.

But now it's time to come down, so Marisol looks away from the crowd and at the branch under her feet.

Her heart thunders in her chest.

It's a long way down.

Even though the treetop is only in Marisol's imagination, still . . .

It's a long way down.

Marisol closes her eyes. "You can do it," she says.

But guess what?

She can't.

Someone laughs. Evie, probably.

Marisol *knows* it's her imagination. She can make anything happen that she wants. She can pull the tree out of the ground and fly off into the clouds like a witch, if she wants to. She decides to try it. She tugs and tugs, but the tree won't come loose. *I am trapped here forever,* she thinks. *They will have to call the fire department and they will have to send helicopters to rescue me, just like the helicopters that take Dad to his rig. And I'll have to ride in one of those baskets that dangle back and forth as they try to pull me up. And what if I fall out of that instead?*

"You can't do anything right," Marisol says, grabbing Lumpia and holding her tight.

She opens her eyes. She has a tight feeling in her chest, like a well of tears pushing up to her face. But she doesn't want to cry right now. Instead, she walks to Oz's room quietly, quietly. She leaves his door open a crack because she knows Beans will follow her in eventually.

Oz's laptop is open on his desk. She creeps around the dirty clothes, soccer cleats, and shin guards scattered across the floor and sits in front of the screen. She slips on Oz's headphones. She finds a movie starring Mary Pickford and presses play. A few moments later, Beans wanders in.

After she saw *A Dog's Life*, Marisol wanted to see other silent films. Watching silent movies was like traveling back in time. She saw all kinds of ancient things, like old-timey telephones and big, fancy hats, and dresses with bows tied in back. She thought Oz might like the movies too, but he said they were "super boring." He helped her find lots of them online, though. That's how Marisol discovered Mary Pickford. Mary Pickford was a movie star a long, long time ago, just like Charlie

Chaplin. Once upon a time, Mary Pickford was called "America's sweetheart." Marisol wonders what it's like to be someone's sweetheart. Imagine being a sweetheart to all of America! That sounds like a lot of pressure, in Marisol's opinion.

MARY PICKFORD

When Marisol gets a laptop of her own, she'll watch silent movies in her room. But for now, Oz is her best option. He usually doesn't mind, as long as she doesn't wake him up. No chance of that. A thousand knights on fighting horses could stampede through his room and he still wouldn't wake up.

Marisol increases the volume bit by bit, just enough to hear the music. Every time she turns it up a notch, she makes sure Oz is still asleep. He is.

In the movie, mean boys throw things at Mary Pickford, but it doesn't faze her one bit. She throws things right back at them. She makes fists to show she means business. *Don't even try me*, the fists say.

Marisol wonders what it's like to make fists that say *don't even try me.*

She wonders what it's like to dart up to the front of the class like Evie Smythe and give a report without the paper shaking in your hand.

She wonders what it's like to run into a friendly swarm of strangers, throw your arms open wide, and say, "Here I am!"

She wonders what it's like to be brave.

MEOWS

Even though Marisol falls asleep on Oz's floor, she wakes up in her own bed. Oz is only twelve, but he can carry Marisol back to her room.

Beans wakes her up by licking her elbow. His tongue feels like sandpaper.

"Your tongue feels like sandpaper!" Marisol says. She pulls the covers over her head. She doesn't feel like opening her eyes.

Cats don't give up that easily.

Beans meows.

And meows.

And meows.

And meows.

The meows mean "I'm hungry. Fetch me breakfast, serf!"

Marisol grumbles as she gets out of bed. She's wearing her favorite kitten pajamas. Her black hair is tousled every which way. She grumbles as she brushes out the tangles. She grumbles as she brushes her teeth and washes up. She grumbles as she walks into the kitchen and pours food for Beans.

Beans doesn't even wait until she's finished before he sticks his nose into his bowl. He stops meowing so he can eat.

Her mom is in the living room, lifting a cushion from the couch. The sofa is named Betty

Bigmouth. Betty likes to eat things, such as Mrs. Rainey's phone and all the remote controls. Today Betty coughs up Mrs. Rainey's phone, which is lucky for Mrs. Rainey.

Once Mrs. Rainey has her phone, she sits down at the kitchen table and scrolls through it. There's a cup of coffee on the table. Marisol likes the way coffee smells, even if it tastes like mud.

Marisol sneaks a swig of orange juice straight out of the container. She swears Buster Keaton to secrecy. Then she sits down next to her mother and yawns.

"Mom," Marisol says. "Why do cats have scratchy tongues?"

"Probably to help them with grooming," Mrs. Rainey says, without looking up. "Their tongues are like little combs."

"Why do they have to lick themselves all the time?"

"To keep clean."

"Why do they need to be so clean?"

Mrs. Rainey sighs. Marisol knows she's asking a lot of questions, but how is she supposed to get answers without asking questions?

"Let's look it up," says Mrs. Rainey. Her fingers move over her phone, and her eyes dart here and there. Mrs. Rainey and Marisol have the same kind of eyes—very dark. Practically black. Just like their hair. "Let's see . . ."

Marisol watches Beans. He's already finished eating, and now he's licking his paws. He is the fastest eater Marisol has ever seen.

"It says here that cats groom themselves to clean their fur of potential parasites," Mrs. Rainey says. "According to this article, some cats spend up to fifty percent of their day grooming themselves."

Birds chirp outside. Marisol wonders what kinds of birds they are. She once asked her mom to teach her how to identify the different birds, but there were so many. It was hard to keep up. Marisol knows hummingbirds, blue jays, and crows, but the others are hard to tell apart.

Marisol also wonders if birds have their own names.

Mrs. Rainey stops scrolling. "Here's a riddle for you," she says. "What is one thing that domestic cats can do that big cats can't?"

Marisol studies Beans, as if he'll give her an answer. Instead, he slinks away to the living room.

"I don't know," Marisol says.

"Think about it, and if you don't know by bedtime, I'll tell you the answer."

Mrs. Rainey is sneaky like that.

"Maybe Jada can help me figure it out," Marisol says.

"Maybe," Mrs. Rainey says.

Marisol pauses. "Mom? Can I ask you something?"

Mrs. Rainey puts her phone down. "Of course, anak."

Anak is a Filipino word that means "child." Her mother calls it a term of endearment. Marisol likes the phrase "term of endearment," and she likes being called "anak."

"Did you climb trees when you were a little girl?" Marisol asks.

Mrs. Rainey raises her eyebrows and says, "You have such surprising questions, anak." She smiles. "Yes, I climbed many trees in the Philippines. There was one called the kalachuchi

tree. It was my favorite. Every time I went up,
I felt like I was in a different world." She takes
a sip of her coffee. "Why do you ask?"

"Just wondering," Marisol says.

KaLaCHuCHi
tREE
↙

TO BE ANY ANIMAL

"If you could be any animal, what would you be?" Jada asks. They are lying on Marisol's bed with Beans between them. "Would you be a cat, like Beans?"

It's a good guess. Not only does Marisol have a cat bedspread, cat pillow, four stuffed animal cats, and one real cat, she also has many pairs of cat ears, which sit side by side on her dresser at this very moment.

Her dresser is named Mabel.

But when Marisol imagines herself as a cat, it doesn't seem fun.

Marisol imagines herself as a small dog instead, curled up on a pillow.

Then she imagines herself as a big dog, splashing through the mud.

She thinks of herself as a bee, like the kind in Mr. Zhang's yard, or a mouse, burrowing underground.

Finally she reaches a decision.

"I'd want to be a bird," she says. *If I was a bird, I'd never fall.*

"But birds eat worms."

Marisol considers this. "I'd be a vegetarian," she says.

Marisol can practically feel the air under her wings as she flies over the world.

"What would you be?" Marisol asks.

Jada answers right away. "Elephant." She counts off the reasons on her fingers: "They're big and strong, so no one will mess with me. They don't have any natural predators, which means I won't have to worry about being eaten. The leader of the herd is always a girl. And they love to swim, just like me."

Marisol doesn't like swimming. Her mom signed her and Oz up for lessons once, but Marisol was afraid to put her head underwater, even though there was an instructor standing in the pool with her and a lifeguard on duty. Oz learned to swim right away. Marisol pretended she wasn't jealous, but she was. She sat on the lawn chair with her mom and watched Oz swim back and forth, back and forth.

It doesn't look like fun at all, she told herself.

But it *did* look like fun. All that splashing and jumping and diving.

Maybe one day she'd try again. Maybe.

"You always have the best answers," Marisol says. She hadn't thought about things like predators and being eaten. That's why Jada was a great philosopher. "Maybe I should change mine."

Birds live in trees, after all, and Marisol was the only girl in the whole world who was too afraid to climb a tree.

That's how it felt, anyway.

"Why?" Jada says. "Being a bird is perfect. You could fly over to the savannah to visit me and tell me about the cool stuff you've seen."

Marisol imagines herself as a bird, landing on

Jada's back. She'd be so little and tiny, with bird feet, and Jada would be vast and round and gray. Jada's elephant back would be endless, just like the Gulf of Mexico around Dadhead's oil rig.

It's a funny thought.

"I have an idea," Marisol says. "Let's pretend to be a bird and an elephant for the rest of the day. But we won't tell anyone what we're doing."

"Kiváló!" says Jada, which means "excellent" in Hungarian.

THE BIG, SCARY WILD

When Marisol flies into the living room, Oz is on the couch watching television. He points the remote at her and presses pause. But it doesn't work, because she's flying too fast. If he were an animal at this moment, he would be a sloth. Sloths are known as the world's laziest animals, because they sleep all day and they move very, very slowly. Really, sloths aren't lazy at all—they move slowly because that's the best way for them to survive in the big, scary wild.

Sometimes, sloths look like they're sleeping even when they're awake.

Zzzz?

When Jada stands in front of him and raises her trunk, he shoos her away, so she lumbers to the back door. Marisol follows.

It's a bazillion degrees outside again, but they don't mind. Wild animals have to survive in all kinds of environments.

Jada lumbers to Peppina. Every now and then she stops to raise her trunk and trumpet as

Marisol skips from one side to the other, flitting like a bird.

Marisol moves quickly, like a proper bird, so she makes it to the tree first.

She stares at booster branch. She looks up. Her tiny bird heart goes *thump, thump, thump.*

Marisol drops her wings and sighs.

Some bird, she says to herself.

SomE BiRd.

MARISOL SOLVES THE RIDDLE

It's ten o'clock at night when Marisol realizes her mother forgot to tell her the answer to the riddle—What can domestic cats do that big cats can't?—and Marisol forgot to ask. But she doesn't want to ask now, because then Mrs. Rainey will know she's up past her bedtime.

Unfortunately, when Marisol's mind gets stuck on something, it's hard to get *unstuck*.

She looks at Beans. Marisol's bed is in a corner, and Beans likes to curl between Marisol and the wall.

At the moment he is half awake and half asleep. His head is up, but his eyes are closed. Nacho, Banana Split, Lumpia, and Pot Roast all have their eyes open. Mostly because their eyes don't close.

"What is something you can do that big cats can't do?" Marisol asks Beans.

☑ Big cats groom.
☑ Small cats groom.
☑ Big cats pounce.
☑ Small cats pounce.
☑ Big cats jump.
☑ Small cats jump.

Marisol rolls over on her side and scratches behind Beans's ears. It's one of his favorite things. It makes him purr every time.

Marisol listens to the light rumble of his purring.

Maybe it will help me fall asleep, she thinks.

She closes her eyes.

What makes cats purr? she wonders.

Then her eyes fly open and she smiles wide, wide. She has solved the riddle.

"I have solved the riddle!" she announces to her mother in the morning.

Mrs. Rainey is already in the hallway, dressed and wearing lipstick, which means she is going somewhere. "What riddle?" she says. "I was about to wake you up. Go get your clothes on, so we're not late."

Her mother already forgot about the riddle!

Maybe forgetfulness runs in the family, because Marisol can't remember where they're supposed to be going this morning.

"About the cats," Marisol says.

Beans walks up behind them, meowing for his breakfast, like always. Marisol prepares it for him, then sits at the table. Oz is awake, which is unusual because it's nine o'clock in the morning. His hair is a black, tangled mess, and there's a half-eaten bowl of cereal in front of him. He looks a lot like Beans at bedtime—half awake, half asleep.

Then Marisol remembers: Oz has sleepover soccer camp this weekend. He won't be home until Sunday.

Mrs. Rainey is in the living room, lifting the throw pillows and shoving her hands in Betty's mouth. Marisol doesn't have to ask what she's doing, because she already knows that she's looking for her phone again.

Oz never loses his phone. It's practically attached to his hand.

Marisol doesn't have a phone yet.

"Don't you want to know the answer?" Marisol says.

"The answer to what?" Mrs. Rainey replies. Now she's in the kitchen, picking up the dish towel by the sink. She pats the back pockets of her shorts for the millionth time.

"The riddle."

Oz looks up from his cereal bowl. "What riddle?"

Marisol repeats it for him.

"That's easy," Oz says, right away. But then he doesn't offer up the answer, because he doesn't actually know it.

"Purr!" Marisol says. "That's the answer. Right, Mom?"

But Mrs. Rainey has disappeared down the hall, still on the hunt.

Doesn't matter anyway.

Marisol knows she's right.

NOT FRIENDS

The soccer camp is being held at the high school. On the way there, Marisol secretly crosses her fingers in her lap. She hopes that they'll drop Oz off in the bus circle and go right back home. But—much to Marisol's horror—Mrs. Rainey pulls Charlie into a parking spot.

Charlie is the name of Mrs. Rainey's sedan.

Oz unbuckles like lightning, hoisting his overnight bag over his shoulder and practically falling out of the car in his hurry. Marisol stays put and surveys the parking lot. Lots of parents are dropping off their kids. She scans the area for Evie Smythe. Evie wears bright colors, like neon green and hot pink, so she's usually easy to spot. And she also wears fox ears. *Not* cat ears, Evie is all too happy to remind everyone.

Marisol doesn't see her, but that doesn't mean she isn't there.

It would be nice if Evie and Marisol were friends, just like Stu and Oz.

But they are *not* friends.

"Hurry up, Marisol," Mrs. Rainey says.

"Can I wait in the car?" Marisol asks. Her fingers are still crossed.

There are dangers to waiting in the car. What if her mom takes too long and the car door won't open and Marisol is trapped inside? What if a maniac steals the car with Marisol in the backseat? What if the brakes malfunction and Charlie rolls into traffic?

Marisol is willing to take her chances.

Anything is better than facing Evie.

Evie Smythe

"No," Mrs. Rainey says. "It's too hot. Now hurry up."

Marisol grumbles and unbuckles. She follows her mother and brother toward the long table that has been set up near the entrance to the school. She looks around for Evie while Oz gets signed in. She wants to be prepared, even though she's never quite prepared. Evie always manages to pounce just when she isn't looking.

Like at this very moment.

"Oh hi, *Marisol*." Evie always says *Marisol* like it's the most boring name in the whole entire universe.

Marisol turns around to face her.

Stu is there, but he doesn't say hello to Marisol, because he's too busy heading for Oz so they can talk about the amazing weekend they'll have.

"My dad is taking me fishing tomorrow," Evie says. She crosses her arms. She is wearing turquoise today. "Just me and him. He's gonna show me how to catch a trout, and then we're gonna eat it for dinner."

This sounds like a perfectly nice thing to say, but Marisol knows better, because she knows Evie Smythe. The words that come out of Evie Smythe's mouth are like darts.

Last year all the students in Mrs. Ruby's class had to give a report on someone in their family. Mrs. Ruby said it didn't even have to be someone you're related to, just someone who you think of as your family.

"Family can mean different things to different people," Mrs. Ruby explained. "And families can be very different from one another."

Marisol knew that already, because she was the only one in her class who had a parent from another country and relatives who lived on the other side of the world. She thought about giving a report about that, but she decided to talk about her dad instead. Some of the kids thought it was interesting that he lived on an oil rig and took a helicopter to work. They even asked questions, which made her feel less nervous. Felix Powell asked if she ever missed her dad when he was away. If Marisol had known then what she knows now, she wouldn't have said anything. But at the time, she answered yes, because that was the truth.

When Evie heard that, she knew just what kind of darts to throw at Marisol.

Here she goes now:

"My dad is a great fisherman," Evie says. The dart sails and lands. *Thwack!* Evie tilts her head to the side. "Has *your* dad ever taken *you* fishing?"

Within two seconds, Marisol has a speech in her head: *Yes, Evie, my dad takes me fishing all the time. We caught twelve trout once. They were almost bigger than our boat. We ate them until we were so full we exploded. My dad also takes me to the amusement park, and to Audubon Zoo, and to the library every weekend. He flies in from the rig on a helicopter just so he can do all these things. Does your dad fly on helicopters, Evie? Well? Does he?*

Instead, Marisol says, "No."

She doesn't want to tell a lie.

THE CLAW

Evie has a way of niggling into Marisol's head and not letting go. As Marisol and Mrs. Rainey drive away from the high school, Marisol thinks about all the things she could have said to Evie. She could have told her how her dad calls her "Scraps," or how he tells corny jokes all the time. *Does* your *dad tell jokes, Evie? Well? Does he?*

"We should start our girls' weekend with a girls' lunch," Mrs. Rainey says, interrupting

Marisol's train of thought. She smiles in the rearview mirror. "Me and my little anak."

Marisol is in the backseat. She leans forward. She loves when she gets her mom all to herself, especially if it involves going out to lunch.

"Can we go to Dazzo's?"

Dazzo's is her favorite restaurant. They have the best nachos in the whole world. And there's a claw machine.

"Okay," Mrs. Rainey says. "But you're not playing the claw until after we eat."

Marisol orders chicken nachos every time they go to Dazzo's. For her drink, she gets Hi-C

Orange. Not all restaurants have Hi-C Orange, but Dazzo's does.

Mrs. Rainey orders a hamburger and onion rings, but she can't finish everything on her plate.

"If Dad were here, he'd say you eat like a bird," Marisol says, balancing a slice of chicken on her chip before popping it in her mouth.

"That's because your dad has never seen birds eat," says Mrs. Rainey. "They have very healthy appetites. It would make more sense to say, 'You eat like a crocodile,' because crocodiles can go a whole year without eating if they have to."

"A whole *year*?" Marisol says. "Don't they get hungry?"

"They have a very unique metabolism."

METaBOLISM: THE PROCESS THat changES FOOD INto ENERgy.

The waitress arrives to give them the bill, and Marisol's mind immediately switches from crocodiles to the claw machine. Marisol doesn't want to wait for her mom to pay the check.

"Can I go play the claw now?" Marisol asks.

"You can play on the way out," Mrs. Rainey says. "Be patient."

Mrs. Rainey reaches across the table and places two dollars in front of Marisol. That means she will get four chances to play. But they still have to wait for the waitress to come back.

Finally it's time to go.

The official name of the claw machine is the Comfort Zone, because it only has plush stuffed animals in it. Marisol hurries ahead, clutching her two dollars, making a beeline for the faded Comfort Zone sign. She peers inside the claw machine at the mounds and mounds of stuffed animals. There is a one-eyed cat in the corner.

"Don't worry," Marisol says to the cat.

Marisol is excellent at the claw machine.

Nacho and Banana Split were both rescued from Dazzo's claw machine. Once Marisol rescued a floppy dog, which she gave to Jada. Jada named him Cornelius, after an intellectual named Cornelius Golightly, PhD.

CORNeLiuS
goLigHtLy,
PhD.
← teacHeR and
civiL RigHts
activist

"Who are you trying for?" says Mrs. Rainey, who has appeared next to her.

Marisol steers the claw to the back corner and lowers it down. The claw snags on the cat's ear but doesn't pick him up.

"The cat in the corner." Marisol positions the claw for her second attempt.

"It only has one eye."

"I know," Marisol says. "That's why I want him."

But she misses him on the second try. And the third.

The one-eyed cat looks at her.

You're my only hope, the cat says.

"Don't worry," says Marisol.

HI-C

Marisol rescues the one-eyed cat from Dazzo's claw machine on her fourth and final attempt. The cat sits on her lap on the way home. She names him Hi-C.

That night she introduces Hi-C to Dadhead.

"This is Hi-C," Marisol says, holding him up to the camera. "I won him from the claw at Dazzo's."

"He only has one eye, Scraps," Dadhead says.

"I know," says Marisol. "That's why I like him."

"What'd you have to eat?" Dadhead rubs his belly. "Salad with lots of radishes?"

Marisol scrunches her nose. Dadhead knows how much she hates radishes. It's her least favorite food.

Bitter Radish →

What'd we ever do to you?

"Gross," Marisol says. She pauses. "Have you ever been fishing, Dad?"

"Sure," Dadhead says. "But not lately. Why?"

"Maybe you can take me fishing sometime," Marisol says.

Mrs. Rainey turns to look at her quizzically. "What makes you want to go fishing?"

Marisol shrugs.

"I can take you fishing next time I'm home,"

Dadhead replies. "But I should warn you, it's pretty boring. Mostly you just sit and stare."

"I'm good at sitting and staring," Marisol says. And that's true. Sometimes she gets so lost in her imagination that she sits and stares for a really long time. Only, her mind isn't sitting still at all.

"I don't think I have a rod and reel, but I'm sure we can borrow one," Dadhead says.

"If we catch trout, can we cook them for dinner?" Marisol asks.

"I don't think your mom wants the house to smell like trout."

Mrs. Rainey nods. "That is correct. I do *not* want the house to smell like trout."

"If we go fishing, we should bring some music to listen to," Dadhead says. "Something *catchy*." He pauses. "Get it? Something *catchy*?"

Marisol knows what her mother is going to say before she even opens her mouth. She decides to say it instead.

"Good one, Will."

Her parents laugh.

Marisol does, too.

PICKFORD & ATHENA

Silent movies don't have sound, so the directors used title cards to help tell the story. Marisol and Jada decide to make their own silent movie. Mrs. Rainey gives them poster board and markers from her emergency classroom supply closet to make their title cards.

"Let's make a movie about a bird who goes on adventures with an elephant," Marisol suggests.

They're on the living room floor. There are poster board and markers scattered everywhere.

Mrs. Rainey is worried that they'll get marker on her carpet, but she doesn't want them to use the table, because she worries they'll get marker on the table.

"We need to come up with names for our characters," Jada says. She's holding a blue marker with the cap still on. She taps it against her chin.

"My name will be Pickford," Marisol says proudly.

"I'm Athena," Jada says.

They create their first title card.

Now they need a plot. It doesn't take long for them to come up with one.

This is their story line: Pickford and Athena need to defeat an evil human-fox who wears neon and turquoise. The evil human-fox is called

because fire shoots out of her mouth every time she talks.

Queen Firebeak has kidnapped Hi-C and escaped into the forest, and now they have no idea how to find her. They rush outside, into the summer sun.

Jada races to Peppina. Up Jada goes. Past booster. All the way to knobby.

Marisol's heart pounds the whole time.

Her feet are rooted to the ground.

Sweat drips down her back.

Jada stops, one branch past knobby. Marisol can barely see her between the leaves.

"I've got Hi-C, Pickford!" Jada yells. "I'll push Queen Firebeak out of the tree so you can capture her! Are you ready?"

Marisol shouts, "Ready!" and she runs to Peppina.

She opens her arms wide so she can catch Queen Firebeak, but to be honest, she doesn't really want to play anymore.

Elephants don't climb trees, she thinks.

I'm supposed to be a bird, she thinks.

She knows what Jada would say: *Who cares if elephants don't* really *climb trees? For today, they can.*

But Marisol can't fly. She can't even climb.

Not on any day.

HER OWN SHADOW

Stu's dad brings Oz home on Sunday. Marisol crosses her fingers again because she doesn't want to see Evie, but she gets lucky because Evie isn't even in the car. Marisol knows this because she and Jada spy from the living room window while Mrs. Rainey unloads Mr. Gurgle, the dishwasher.

"I bet Evie and her dad didn't even go fishing," Jada says as they watch Oz get out of the car. "She probably made the whole thing up."

When Oz barrels through the front door—smelling sweaty and gross—they follow him to the kitchen. He tosses his bags on the floor, makes a million sandwiches, and tells Mrs. Rainey all about soccer camp—who made goals, who didn't make goals, who threw up after practice. Marisol and Jada are listening, too, perched on the kitchen island, but they can hardly keep track. They don't understand soccer. They don't understand football, baseball, or basketball, either. If they were to make a list of their favorite things—and they have, many times—sports would not be on it. They don't even like doing sports at school. Getty Elementary School has PE classes on Tuesdays and Thursdays, and neither Marisol nor Jada like Tuesdays or Thursdays for this very reason.

To Play Basketball
like Jada:
1. Dribble ball twice.
2. Watch ball bounce
   away.

To jump rope like Marisol:
1. Don't.

When Oz stops to take a breath, Marisol says, "Soccer sounds boring."

She doesn't say it in a mean way.

She isn't trying to make fun of him or soccer.

She's just stating a personal opinion.

But he takes a bite of his sandwich and makes a huffy noise at her. It's a noise that says, *You're one to talk.*

"What do you know?" Oz says, with his mouth full. "You're scared of your own shadow."

There is a twist in the center of Marisol's chest.

"That's not a very nice thing to say to your sister," Mrs. Rainey says. Oz left crumbs on the kitchen counter and she's wiping them away with a paper towel.

At least I clean up my own crumbs, Marisol

thinks. *No one has to pick up after me.*

"So what?" Oz says. He shrugs with one shoulder. "It's true."

As Oz walks back toward his room, holding the last of his turkey sandwich, Jada says, "She should be afraid of *your* shadow, because of how stupid it looks!"

"Jada, that's not very nice," Mrs. Rainey says.

"Lo siento, Mrs. Rainey," Jada says, which means "I'm sorry" in Spanish.

Jada turns to Marisol and nudges her arm.

"You want to go outside and keep working on our movie?" Jada asks.

But Marisol is in no mood for Peppina or Queen Firebeak. "Let's get Ginny and Bunny instead," she says.

Jada nods. They walk together to the garage,

which is where Ginny lives. Bunny is already outside, leaning against the Raineys' front porch.

When they're far enough away from Mrs. Rainey, Jada leans toward Marisol and whispers, "Just so you know, I meant what I said about your stupid brother."

They giggle.

GINNY, BUNNY, AND DAGGERS

Ginny and Bunny are the names of Marisol's and Jada's bicycles. Ginny belongs to Marisol, and it has a red banana seat. Bunny belongs to Jada, and it has a pink banana seat. Bunny also has a basket and bell. Marisol is secretly jealous about this, but she never says anything.

They take the same route every time they ride.

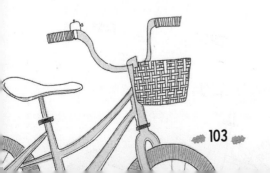

Marisol loves taking trips with Ginny, even when it's blazing hot outside. She likes the way the wind whips through her hair and blows it all around, and she's proud of how fast she can go. She didn't think she'd ever be able to go fast, because she was scared the first time she got on her bicycle, even though it had training wheels.

She probably would never have learned at all if it hadn't been for her dad. He came home one weekend and surprised her with her first bike. This was last year, when they lived in the apartment. Her dad spent all day teaching her how to balance. She wanted to give up many times, but she only had one weekend with him and she didn't want to ruin it.

"Once you learn how to ride a bike, you never forget," he told her.

And he was right. She's been able to ride ever since.

Now she's going even faster than Jada, and she's almost at the house with the red door, which is where they'll turn the corner.

That's when Marisol slows down.

Slow, slow.

She drags her sneaker on the ground.

You can't just fly right into the face of danger. You need to think it through first.

Marisol waits for Jada to catch up.

She eyes the chain-link fence across the street.

Her heart goes *tha-thump, tha-thump*.

Jada stops Bunny right next to Ginny. They stare at the fence.

"Ready?" Jada says.

"Ready."

They push themselves past the fence on their tiptoes.

Tha-thump. Tha-thump.

A bead of sweat trickles down Marisol's back. It tickles, but she doesn't move or squirm. Forward, forward. Slow, slow.

Closer, closer.

Daggers*
tHE
GERMan
ShePheRD

*ReaL
namE
unKnown

"Remember, no eye contact," Jada says, even though she's looking right at him.

Oz told them once that you should never make eye contact with a dog, because dogs think that's a threat. Every time they see Daggers, Marisol and Jada remind themselves not to make eye contact, but they always do. In Marisol's mind, the only thing worse than making eye contact is *not* making eye contact. What if Daggers does something vicious and she doesn't see it coming? She looks at his nose instead of his eyes.

But his nose is just as scary, because it's close to his teeth.

Daggers growls, low and rumbly, then sits and stares at them.

Marisol and Jada inch forward.

You're not supposed to run away from dogs, either, because they'll chase you.

That's something else Oz taught them.

Once they've inched their bikes all the way to safety, they stand on the pedals and pump their legs to gain speed. Marisol feels like she's flying. The air lifts her hair. She's flying, flying.

"We made it!" Jada says.

Marisol lets go of the handlebars and throws her hands up in celebration.

But only for two seconds.

LO SIENTO

Marisol and Jada ride their bikes for a long time before they finally coast back to Marisol's house. The back of Marisol's neck is sweaty, but she doesn't mind. She likes the way the wind feels against her skin. When they reach her house, Marisol pulls into the driveway, and Jada follows behind. They park Ginny and Bunny near the front porch, put their kickstands down, and walk inside to the glorious air-conditioning.

Marisol gulps down a tall glass of water. She

felt happy and free when she was riding her bike, but now that she's home again, she thinks about what Oz said. *You're scared of your own shadow.*

Jada finishes her water and says, "Let's work on the next scene of our movie before I have to go home."

Jada rushes outside. Marisol follows her, but suddenly she doesn't feel like making movies anymore. Jada hops onto booster branch and up she goes. The higher Jada climbs in Peppina, the less Marisol feels like playing.

Marisol slows her pace across the yard. When she finally reaches Peppina, she looks up, and Jada looks down. Jada is perched on knobby branch.

"I don't feel like it anymore," Marisol says.

Jada swings her legs. Comfortable, comfortable. Not scared at all.

Why do I have to be scared of everything all the time? No one else is, Marisol thinks.

"Why not?" Jada asks.

"I just don't want to," Marisol says. She crosses her arms. She doesn't know why she's annoyed, but she is. And Jada hasn't done anything wrong, but Marisol doesn't care. "And elephants don't even climb trees, so I don't know why you're up there in the first place!"

Jada frowns. "Why are you being a grouchy grandpa?"

That's one of their secret codes. Just like the words they speak in other languages.

One day, right after they became best friends, they saw a grouchy man waiting in the pickup line at school. His face was scrunched tight, tight, like a raisin. He seemed very unhappy to be sitting in his car. "Look at that grouchy grandpa!" Jada said, and they laughed and laughed. Soon enough they were laughing at how much they were laughing.

But right now Marisol doesn't feel like laughing. Marisol wants to repeat again and again that elephants don't climb trees and it's stupid to think of an elephant in a tree and they can't really make a movie anyway because they don't even have a camera and they need to make new title cards, but that's not really what she wants to say, and who cares about that anyway, so she doesn't say anything for a few seconds.

"I'm not being a grouchy grandpa!" Marisol says. She knows that she sounds like a baby having a tantrum, but she doesn't care. She's mad at Peppina for being in her backyard. She's mad at Jada for not being afraid. She's mad at Oz for saying she was scared of her shadow. Mostly, though, she's mad at herself for being the only kid in the entire world who is too afraid to climb a tree.

Jada frowns at her. Marisol looks away.

It's not Jada's fault, and she knows that.

Marisol uncrosses her arms and says, "Lo siento, Jada. I guess I just don't want you to go home." This is a half truth. She decides to tell the whole truth. "And I'm mad at myself for not climbing Peppina."

Marisol doesn't ask Jada to come down, but she does anyway. She lands next to Marisol, on both feet.

"It's okay," Jada says.

That's the thing about best friends.

You can tell the whole truth, if you want to.

PITY PARTY

There are only ten minutes left before Jada has to go home. Marisol is sitting on the ground under booster branch, snatching up pieces of grass and tossing them in the air for no reason. She wishes she had a huge banana split with heaps of vanilla ice cream and a zillion cherries on top. That would make the day a little better.

Jada is in the tree again. She climbs to the next branch and the next, while Marisol leans her head back and watches. Finally Jada stops.

She shields her eyes with her hands and sits up very straight.

"I see the window to your kitchen. And Mr. Zhang's beehouse!" Jada calls down. "But don't worry, there are no bees loose." She makes a telescope with her hands. "Mrs. Blumenthal just opened her curtains!"

Jada is quiet for a while, probably looking for new things to report. Marisol adds sprinkles to her imaginary banana split and an extra scoop of vanilla, just because. Then Jada makes a noise, like a half-startled squeal of delight.

"Marisol!" Jada says. "You won't believe what's up here!"

Marisol stands. Blades of grass are stuck to her legs. She squints up at Jada, who has scooted closer to Peppina's trunk.

"It's a bird's nest!" Jada is whispering, but Marisol can still hear her.

Marisol feels as bright as the sun. She's never seen a bird's nest in real life before. "Really?"

"Yes!" Jada says. "There are no birds in it, but it's definitely a bird's nest." She pauses. "There's all kinds of stuff tangled up with the twigs! There's even a pink ribbon! I wonder if it's from our balloons?"

Jada and Marisol got balloons a few weeks ago at the spring festival.

Marisol imagines a bird plucking the ribbon in its beak and soaring high above Getty, Louisiana, maybe all the way to the Gulf of Mexico and back, before landing in Peppina and weaving the ribbon into the nest for its babies.

She wishes she could see it.

She wraps her arms under booster branch. All she has to do is lift herself up. She knows that. She's seen Jada and Oz do it millions of times. Easy-peasy.

She cranes her neck and looks at Jada.

"There's a feather in here, Marisol!" says Jada. "A tiny little feather! I wonder what kind of birds lived here? We should ask your mom!"

Marisol's heart thumps. *Tha-thump. Tha-thump.*

She wants to climb Peppina. She really does. She puts her sneaker against the trunk. But she imagines herself slipping, losing her balance, tumbling to the ground, hitting her head. The entire story unfolds in her mind, like a silent movie where the title card says:

DOWN
SHE GOES!

She drops her arms.

I wish I was a bird, she thinks. *But I'm just Marisol.*

That night Marisol gathers Nacho, Banana Split, Lumpia, Pot Roast, and Hi-C and tucks them into her bed. She doesn't feel like watching an old movie, because she has decided to have a pity party. All the cats are invited—stuffed and real.

A pity party is when you spend time feeling sorry for yourself. Marisol's pity parties always happen at night, when she is by herself and it is very quiet and everyone else is asleep.

Nacho and Hi-C are tucked on Marisol's left side. Banana Split, Lumpia, and Pot Roast are on her right. Beans is curled at her feet, on top of the covers. Sometimes Beans makes it hard to sleep because he lies on top of the comforter and Marisol can't pull up the blankets without waking him.

Now that everyone is in place and it's dark-dark outside and everything is quiet, the pity party can begin.

Yes, Marisol is feeling quite sorry for herself.

But that's the thing about pity parties: they aren't satisfying if you don't feel at least a little sad for yourself.

NEW DAY

Marisol sleeps later than usual in the morning, because pity parties are exhausting. But when she finally stretches and sits up, with Beans meowing and meowing and meowing, she feels better.

"It's a new day," she says to Beans.

Beans doesn't care. He just wants to eat breakfast.

Her other cats are scattered all over the bed. Marisol wonders if they rummaged around while she was asleep. She knows they probably didn't, but it's nice to imagine anyway.

Mrs. Rainey is in the living room, reading a book.

"Good morning!" she says to Marisol. "You slept in. Did you stay up late?"

Marisol prepares a bowl of food for Beans.

"Maybe," Marisol says. "I'm not sure what time it was."

Half-truth. She had looked at the clock several times. The last time she looked, it was 12:19. But it's not an all-the-way fib, because she's honestly not sure what time she fell asleep.

Now it's ten in the morning. Jada usually comes over around lunchtime, so Marisol decides to sit with her mother until then.

"Jada found a bird's nest in the magnolia tree, but the birds were gone," Marisol says. "What kind of birds made it, do you think?"

"There are many possibilities," Mrs. Rainey says. "Cardinals, maybe."

Marisol imagines the nest full of cardinals. She imagines them singing a song about the ribbon they found. Maybe they sing about Mr. Zhang's bees, or how excited they are to see flowers in the spring.

What Birds are Really saying.

"We should get a bird for a pet," Marisol suggests. "A parrot!"

Mrs. Rainey lays the book on her lap. "Parrots are the only birds that can eat with their feet, you know."

"Then we should definitely get one."

"But they live a really long time. Fifty years, even. That's a big commitment."

"Hm," says Marisol. "We could get a different bird. One that sings."

"Maybe we should focus on Beans for now," Mrs. Rainey says.

Beans saunters into the room, as if he knew they'd be talking about him. He stops to lick his paws.

"Maybe," Marisol says. "But he can't sing or eat with his feet."

"Neither can your brother, but we keep *him*," Mrs. Rainey says.

Marisol shrugs. "If you want to trade Oz for a parrot, I wouldn't mind."

MAYBE TOMORROW

When Jada comes over, she's sweaty from riding her bike. She comes inside the cool air-conditioning and asks Marisol what she wants to do.

Marisol closes the front door and makes her way to the back door. Jada follows.

"I want to see the bird's nest," Marisol announces.

She has decided. The pity party is over. It's a new day, and now she knows she wants to climb

Peppina. She wants to know what it's like to be in another world, like how her mom felt when she was a girl and she climbed the kalachuchi trees in the Philippines. She wants to know what the bird's nest looks like with the ribbon inside. She wants to see the feather, too. She wants to know how it feels to see Mrs. Blumenthal's house and Mr. Zhang's bees from way up high. She wants to know what it feels like to be perched in a tree like a bird.

Marisol opens the back door.

"You mean . . . you're going to climb Peppina?" Jada asks as they walk into the yard. Peppina is waiting for them.

"Yes." Marisol stands very straight and proud. She has decided. Yes, she will climb Peppina today.

"Hourra!" Jada says, which means "hooray" in French.

They race to Peppina together, with Jada calling, "Hourra! Hourra!" all the way.

Peppina looks tall. Like always.

Peppina is a tree. Like always.

Peppina doesn't have arms to catch Marisol when she falls. Like always.

Jada is already on booster branch. She pauses and looks down as Marisol looks up. Marisol had planned to leap onto Peppina straightaway, but her feet are stuck.

"Aren't you coming?" Jada asks—softly, not meanly.

Marisol swallows.

Maybe.

"Yes," she says.

Jada taps Peppina's bark and then looks down

at Marisol. "It's okay if you don't climb the tree, Marisol. Socrates says we should always know ourselves."

"What does that mean?" Sometimes it annoys Marisol when Jada says stuff like that.

Jada shrugs. "Maybe you're just not a person who likes to climb trees. Maybe you're a ground person. You don't *have* to climb Peppina."

"Yeah, but . . ."

"But what?"

"I *want* to. I'm just . . ."

"Just what?"

Marisol takes a deep breath. Jada is her best friend, and she knows she can tell Jada anything. But sometimes it's hard to say things out loud, even to best friends.

But Marisol says it anyway.

Jada nods. She knew this all along, of course. And even though Jada isn't afraid of climbing trees, she knows what it's like to be scared. Who doesn't?

"I'm scared of falling," Marisol says.

Jada cranes her neck and looks up into the canopy of Peppina, as if she's seeing it for the first time. She looks down, to the roots. She looks at Marisol. She swings both legs over booster branch and jumps down the way she always does. Booster branch isn't that far off the ground, after all, even if it feels like miles to Marisol.

Jada brushes her hands off. She stands next to Marisol, so they're side by side, and opens her arms like she's giving Marisol a bear hug, even though that's not what she's doing at all.

"Ready?" Jada says.

"Ready for what?" Marisol asks.

"To climb Peppina," Jada says, nodding at her open arms. "If you fall, I'll catch you."

Marisol looks at Jada's arms.

She looks at Peppina.

She looks at booster branch.

Trees can't catch people.

But best friends can.

Marisol puts her sneaker on Peppina's trunk,

the way she's seen Jada and Oz do a hundred times.

She checks to make sure Jada is behind her, and she is—of course, she is.

Marisol takes a deep breath and pulls herself up.

Jada gives her a little boost, even though she doesn't need it, because now Marisol is sitting on the branch. She keeps both palms flat on the bark to steady herself.

"Hourra! Hourra!" Jada cries. She waves her arms in the air and spins and spins, saying it again and again. Then she remembers she's an elephant, so she raises her trunk in triumph. When she's done, she stands still and beams. She opens her arms again. "Ready to go up? The nest is way past knobby branch."

Marisol is holding on tight. She looks down at Jada. Her heart races.

Marisol tries to relax her hands—slowly, slowly—but her whole body is tense and scared.

"I want to come down," Marisol says. Her voice shakes. But she manages to smile anyway. "Maybe tomorrow I'll go higher."

maybE.

THE PERFECT TREE

The next morning, Marisol gets dressed as soon as she wakes up. Beans follows her to the kitchen and eats his breakfast. Mrs. Rainey is pouring coffee into her favorite yellow mug. She's humming "You Are My Sunshine."

"I'm going in the backyard," Marisol says with as much conviction as she can. She stands up tall, even though her heart is *tha-thump*ing. "Will you watch me?"

Mrs. Rainey glances at the window over the

sink. You can see Peppina directly through that window, branches and all.

"I'm going to climb the tree," Marisol announces. She lifts her chin.

Mrs. Rainey raises her eyebrows. "Do you want me to come outside?"

"No, just watch from the window," Marisol says.

"Okay," Mrs. Rainey says. She carries her mug to the sink and blows on her coffee while Marisol goes outside.

It's already hot, even though it's not even nine o'clock yet. Marisol stops to make sure Mrs. Rainey is at the window. She is. Marisol waves, and Mrs. Rainey waves back.

Marisol marches across the yard, like a soldier going into battle. When she reaches the trunk, she looks up and says, "Hello, Peppina."

But not like she's greeting a bowl of cold oatmeal.

More like she's making a new friend.

Marisol turns and waves to her mother again.

She lifts herself onto booster branch, using her sneaker to push herself up.

The trunk feels bumpy and earthy under her hands.

Her heart goes *tha-thump*.

A bead of sweat drips down her forehead and into her eye.

She blinks it away and keeps going.

Once she's seated, she takes a breath and waves to her mom.

Her mom waves back.

Marisol pulls herself up to the next branch and the next.

For a second she worries about falling.

But only for a second.

She keeps going. It's not as hard as she thought it would be.

She even looks down, and it doesn't look so bad.

Her heart still *tha-thumps*, but more quietly now.

She wipes sweat away with her sleeve.

She looks down again and sees knobby branch under her feet.

Marisol can see her mother through Peppina's shiny green leaves. Mrs. Rainey waves and waves.

Marisol isn't ready to wave back yet. She needs both her arms and hands, because now she's going up and up. There! She sees the nest. It's tucked in a nook in the branches. She scoots forward. Scoots and scoots. Slowly, carefully.

There's the feather. It's red. Her mother was right! This nest probably belonged to a family of cardinals. Marisol lifts the red feather carefully, runs her fingers across it, and puts it into her pocket.

Maybe one day I'll see a nest with baby birds, she thinks. *Maybe.*

She feels like she's part of another world way up here.

She can see Mr. Zhang's yard. His beehive sits right in the center. Only it really is more like a beehouse, with a pitched roof and everything. And there's Mrs. Blumenthal, watering her plants. She can even see Mrs. Blumenthal's neighbor, the man with the salt-and-pepper beard. Marisol can never remember his name, but there he is, fiddling with his lawn mower. He has no idea that there's a spy in the tree at the Rainey house.

She closes her eyes.

She's still a little afraid, but mostly she feels brave. She takes a deep, deep breath and thinks she smells magnolias, even though they won't bloom again until next spring.

Maybe it's just my imagination, she thinks.

Things that aren't her imagination: The leaves all around. The branch underneath. The nest nearby. The feeling in her chest that swells and swells, but it's not pity. It's pride!

Maybe, maybe, I'll stay right here until Jada arrives.

She imagines Jada's face when she sees her up there.

She imagines how happy her mother will be when she gives her the feather.

She imagines Peppina, all her branches and bark, thinking: *Finally, you came.*

"You are the perfect tree," she whispers.

Be on the lookout
for more
adventures with
Marisol!